Mr. Bear's Vacation

DEBI GLIORI

ORCHARD BOOKS   NEW YORK

With lots of love to Caroline and Dave
and Alice and Oliver and Holly—
crossing continents and turning
their lives into an adventure—D.G.

Orchard Books, A Grolier Company
95 Madison Avenue, New York, NY 10016

Printed in Hong Kong/China
Book design by Nancy Goldenberg
The text of this book is set in 16 point Veljovic Medium.
    The illustrations are watercolor.

        10 9 8 7 6 5 4 3 2 1
                Library of Congress Cataloging-in-Publication Data

            Gliori, Debi.
                Mr. Bear's vacation / by Debi Gliori.—1st American ed.
                p.   cm.
                    Summary: When Mr. Bear's relaxing camping trip with his fam-
                    ily turns into a scary nightmare, he decides they need a vaca-
                    tion from their vacation.
                    ISBN 0-531-30255-5 (trade : alk. paper)
                    [1.Vacations Fiction. 2. Camping Fiction.
                    3. Bears Fiction.]
                    I. Title. PZ7.G4889Mv 2000 [E]—dc21 99-35490

"Look, Small, a postcard's
come for you," said Mrs. Bear.
"Lucky Grizzle-Bears—
they're on vacation."

"Can we go on vacation?" said Small Bear. "On a plane? Or a rocket, or a ship, or a train?"

"A vacation," said Mr. Bear, emerging from behind his newspaper. "That's a good idea. How about a tent?"

"What's a tent?" asked Small Bear.

"Wait and see," said Mrs. Bear. "Let's have breakfast first."

After breakfast they all helped
to get ready. Mr. Bear found the tent.
Small Bear found the sleeping bags.
Baby Bear found the maps.

Mrs. Bear organized the food, sunblock, candles, sunglasses, hats, cups, forks, knives, spoons, matches, and Band-Aids. She also made four honey sandwiches, just in case.

By lunchtime they were ready.

"I love vacations," said Small Bear as they set off. "Where are we going?"

"Wait and see," said Mr. Bear, staggering under the weight of the backpack. "It's an adventure."

It was a very long adventure.
First they stopped to change Baby Bear's diaper.

"Are we there yet?" asked Small Bear.
"Not yet," said Mr. Bear.

A little later they stopped to eat their sandwiches.
"When are we going to be there?" asked Small Bear.
"Soon," said Mr. Bear. "Be patient."

A long time later they stopped to look at the map.
"Do you know where we're going?" asked Small Bear.
"Sort of," said Mr. Bear. "Not far now," he added hopefully.

The sun was beginning to slip behind the trees when Mr. Bear finally stopped.

"Here we are," he said, dropping the backpack with a groan.

Small Bear looked around. "Is this a vacation?" she asked suspiciously.

"No!" snapped Mr. Bear. "It's an *adventure*!"

Small Bear's lower lip began to quiver. "Let's go find some wood for the fire," said Mrs. Bear, "and leave Dad and Baby Bear to put up the tent."

Mrs. Bear and Small Bear headed for the woods.

As Baby Bear watched, Mr. Bear unrolled the tent. Several hundred moths flew out. Baby Bear clapped her paws in delight.

"Oh dear," said Mr. Bear. "Poor tent."

Baby Bear looked on in silent wonder as Mr. Bear struggled heroically with the holey tent. Ropes snapped and poles bent, but eventually Mr. Bear succeeded in putting up the tent.

"There," he said. "Just the right size for the four of us."

"Look who I found," said Small Bear, running
back. "Can Flora stay too?"

"We met her family in the woods," sighed
Mrs. Bear. "Mrs. Rabbit-Bunn would've liked them
all to come along, but . . ."

The first stars were just appearing in the sky when the Bear family and their guest sat down to supper.

"Sorry, it's a bit burnt," said Mrs. Bear.

"It's delicious," said Mr. Bear. "This is what vacations are all about: firelight, starlight, and supper in the open air."

Suddenly a large cloud blotted out the stars, and a chill wind began to blow. The Bears huddled around the fire. Flora climbed onto Small Bear's lap.

Mr. Bear rummaged through the backpack. "Oh dear," he said.

"What's the matter?" said Mrs. Bear.

"I forgot to pack the sleeping bags," said Mr. Bear.

Baby Bear began to cry.
Small Bear's lower lip
wobbled dangerously.

"Never mind," sighed Mrs. Bear.
"We'll just huddle together in our
nice warm tent."

But it wasn't much warmer in the nice warm tent.

"Look," said Small Bear, "I can see the stars through the roof."

"Yes," said Mrs. Bear grimly, "and you can feel the wind too."

"What's *that*?" said Mr. Bear.
"What?" said Mrs. Bear.
"That snorting sound,"
whispered Mr. Bear. "Outside,
listen. . . ."
  The Bears fell silent.
Flora's ears twitched.

"Look," said Mrs. Bear in a trembly whisper. "There on the wall."
"AAARGH!" screamed Mr. Bear.
"It's a monster!" wailed Small Bear.
"MoooOOO," said the monster.

Mr. Bear bravely stuck his head out of the tent to investigate. "Oh *dear*!" he said.

"MoooOO SNORT," said the monster, leaning on the tent.

"Quick! Let's go!" yelled Mr. Bear, quickly
putting out the fire, stuffing the little bears
into the backpack, and pulling Mrs. Bear
and Flora after him.
     They sprinted away from
the tent just as it collapsed
under the weight of a
curious cow.

The Bears walked home by moonlight. Just as they were returning Flora to her burrow, a shadow swooped down from the treetops. The Bear family shrieked.

"It's only me," said Mr. Hoot-Toowit. "You're all so *jumpy*—I think you need a vacation."

"We've just had a vacation," said Small Bear.

"Did you have a nice time?" said Mr. Hoot-Toowit.

The Bears smiled a secret smile.
"I think," laughed Mr. Bear, "I think we all need
another vacation to recover from our vacation."